DUCK at the DOOR

Jackie Urbanovic

SCHOLASTIC INC.
New York Toronto London Auckland Sydney
Mexico City New Delhi Hong Kong Buenos Aires

No part of this publication may be reproduced, stored in a retrieval system, or transmitted in any form or by any means, electronic, mechanical, photocopying, recording, or otherwise, without written permission of the publisher. For information regarding permission, write to HarperCollins Children's Books, a division of HarperCollins Publishers, 1350 Avenue of the Americas, New York, NY 10019.

ISBN-13: 978-0-545-15129-0
ISBN-10: 0-545-15129-5

Copyright © 2007 by Jackie Urbanovic. All rights reserved. Published by Scholastic Inc., 557 Broadway, New York, NY 10012, by arrangement with HarperCollins Children's Books, a division of HarperCollins Publishers. SCHOLASTIC and associated logos are trademarks and/or registered trademarks of Scholastic Inc.

18 17 16   11 12 13 14/0

Printed in the U.S.A.   40

First Scholastic printing, March 2009

Typography by Carla Weise

For Susan Dreiband,
my behind-the-scenes co-creator.

With thanks to Jane Resh Thomas, who taught me to write, and to
her writing group for so much laughter and support. To Max Haynes,
who was always willing to share his time and ideas. And, of course,
to the real Irene, Brody, and Scrappy, who inspired this story.

It was a quiet
night until . . .

Thunk, creak, and KNOCK, KNOCK, KNOCK!

SOMEONE IS
OUT THERE!

BUT WHO?

"LET'S GO ASK IRENE!

SHE ALWAYS KNOWS WHAT TO DO."

"Irene!" cried Brody. "Help!
Someone is knocking on our door!"

"It's the middle of the night," said Irene.
"Who could be knocking on our door?"

It's a
DUCK!

Irene brought the duck inside.

"My name is Max," he began. "I was born in the spring, and I loved it. I stayed behind when my flock flew south because I thought I'd love winter too. But it turned out to be COLD and very lonely."

"Winter isn't so bad when you have a warm home," said Irene.

At first Max
had a lot to learn.

In January he learned to use the remote control.
(He enjoyed *Wild Kingdom* and *World Wide Wrestling*.)

In February he
discovered he had
a flair for cooking.

By March he had made
himself right at home.

But by April it was clear that Max had learned too much.

Dakota, Coco, and Jesse Bear
got tired of Max's new recipes.

MAX'S TOFU
SURPRISE!

SHISH KEBOB
À LA MAX

MAX'S SEAWEED
CHOWDER

And Brody
was just tired.

Someone had to talk to Max.

But **WHO**?

Just then Max burst into the room yelling, "Listen to the quacking! My flock has returned! I can't wait to see them."

"Irene, please keep my chef's hat. And Brody, you can have my rubber duckies. I will miss you all so much!"

After many hugs, Max left.

With Max gone, life was ordinary again.

The cats went back to
eating plain cat food.
No one played keep-away
with the remote control.

And Brody didn't have to share his bed.

Life was so quiet that by October, everyone
was happy to hear the sound of quacking.
When there was a knock at the door, everyone
was hoping the same thing.

"MAX!" they shouted with joy.
"Are you staying with us all winter?"
they asked.

"Yes," said Max. "Me and . . .

...MY FLOCK!"

Everyone looked at Irene, hoping she would say something.

But all she could say was

"WELCOME HOME!"